Frankenstein King of the Dead

Book 1.5

Frank vs. The Rat Pack

A Frankenstein King of the Dead Novella

By Josh Hilden

Gorillas with Scissors Press LLC

ISBN-10 : 1514256347

ISBN-13 : 978-1514256343

www.joshhilden.com

Frankenstein King of The Dead Series

Book 0: Pleased to Meet You - (Short Story)

Book 1: Overture of Chaos

Book 1.5: Run & Hyde

Book 2: Transition of Terror

Book 2.5: Frank vs. the rat pack

Book 3: Ballad of Suspense

Table of Contents

Chapter One

Now

In the Air, Onboard Brenda

Below them the world burned, monsters roamed the land, and the dead fed on the flesh of the living. Terror and death was the order of the day for the human race, but for the moment we were safe in the skies above Michigan.

"How are they?" I asked Susan.

Closing the cockpit door behind her when she entered the cockpit, my love breathed a deep sigh of relief. "We've finally got them settled in, all things considered they're doing okay. The ones we rescued from those bastards are in rough shape, some are already presenting signs of serious PTSD, but the girls are taking good care of them," she finished dropping into the copilot's seat.

"How's Andy?" I asked toggling the autopilot and turning my chair to look at Susan. It'd been a long time since I'd seen someone so beautiful and strong in the flesh.

"That is one tough kid," Susan replied. I could see the stress and energy finally draining from her features right before my eyes. It wouldn't be long before she was sound asleep. "He helped me get things situated back there. By the way Frank, what the hell happened to your plane? It looks like someone took a can opener to the back."

I laughed despite myself.

"What's so funny?" Susan asked, her beautiful eyebrow arched.

"You're not too far from the truth," I answered twisting my head to the side and enjoying the sensation of it popping—it'd been a long day. "There were three of them and they messed up Brenda's roof pretty bad in the back."

"Who's Brenda?" Susan asked not even bothering to fight back the snort of laughter escaping her.

"My plane," I muttered feeling heat racing to the surface of my pale skin.

"For everything that makes you unique and

awesome Frank, you're still a guy at heart," she said placing a hand on my knee and grinning. Then she added a little more somberly, "Do you have any idea how long I've dreamed of actually seeing you?"

"I can imagine," I said smiling sadly.

She squeezed my knee. "What's happening Frank? I've been wracking my brain and all of this sounds like something from a really bad disaster porn from the nineties."

"It's much worse than that," I answered straightening myself and placing my hand on top of hers. "It's the end of the world Susan, or it will be if we can't stop it."

"We?" she asked looking and sounding stunned. "What do you mean by 'we' Frank? We're just people."

"I've been alive a long time Susan," I laughed. "This isn't my first rodeo as the saying goes."

"I'm completely confused Frank," she sighed before continuing in a small exhausted voice. "In the last few days I've watched the world become destroyed, fought zombies, watched good friends die, and killed murderous bastards intent on raping and imprisoning innocent people. Please just tell me what's happening."

"I'm not entirely sure Susan, but it's been in motion for longer than I've been alive," I replied then added darkly, "maybe longer than the human species has been around."

Shock filled Susan's face but was quickly covered by a descending veil of cold logic. "Okay, there are things happening no one could have ever imagined. I need those details, but first tell me you can fight this. Tell me we can win. Tell me this isn't the swansong of our species."

"Your species," I said before I could stop myself.

"Don't you ever say that again," Susan said icily pulling her hand from my knee. "I've known you most of my life. If you really love me you will never say you're not human again. You are a man, the best man I've ever known. Never talk down about yourself, not in my presence, not ever."

"I'm sorry," I said looking up and at her. "It's just hard to break a habit of several life times."

"Well try," she said this time allowing warmth to enter her voice. "Now, tell me you have a plan, please."

"I've been working on a plan for more than a

century," I said releasing a breath I wasn't aware I'd been holding. "As to whether I can handle it, well like I said, this isn't my first time fighting supernatural evil."

I paused and thought how I was going to phrase the next part. I didn't get far in my thoughts before Susan stopped them.

"I'm exhausted already and we still have a long trip ahead of us," she said.

"We might have to stop and rest the engines at some point around Lake Superior," I added. "Otherwise the strain of this weather could overheat the thorium reactor and her systems will start shutting down."

She nodded and continued, "I can't sleep though, I'm too on edge." Then she added in a voice I hadn't heard in years, the voice of young Susan, who when she couldn't sleep would call me in the middle of the night, "Tell me a story Frank, tell me a story like you used to and help me sleep." She got up, walked over to me, and curled up on my spacious lap.

Chapter Two

December 1963

Sands Hotel, Las Vegas, Nevada

I blame you for this Vlad, I thought handing the young woman behind the counter three twenties and a ten. You think if you snap your fingers I'll do what you want—that's an abuse of our friendship. I like Vegas but I want to come here on my terms, not yours, old friend. I mean seriously what was so damn urgent that you couldn't haul your butt out here from Europe?

"Thank you Mr. Castle," the attractive young blonde woman said handing me a receipt, a room key, and another slip of paper—this one blue. "As one of our preferred returning customers, management would like to give you a voucher for a hundred dollars in complimentary chips."

"Thank you," I answered smiling. I had to give it to

her she was a professional and neither my voice nor my scars phased her. It probably didn't hurt that I dropped about ten grand a year at the casino. "Is the refrigerator stocked?" I asked a little embarrassed.

"Of course, sir," she answered, the professional smile changing into a genuine grin. "Chef Paul loves it when you're in town, he gets to experiment and order things normally not on the allowed budget. He told me to tell you he has three of those amazing cheesecakes already finished and ready."

I grinned back. In my first trip to the Sands I'm met then Sous Chef Paul and struck up a friendship. He told me once that the cheesecake recipe I'd given him, the one Albert said his mother invented, had gotten him the Head Chef's position.

"That sounds wonderful," I said slipping the papers in my jacket pocket.

"Henry," the woman said, "can you help Mr. Castle with his bags?"

"Of course, Audrey," the handsome, middle aged black man in a bellhop's uniform answered. "How have you been Mr. Castle? It's been a few months since your last visit. Mindy appreciated the Christmas presents you sent for the kids, she has them hidden at her mother's house so the little ones don't sniff them out."

"They grow up fast," I laughed, wincing as he loaded my bags on a cart.

I wanted to tell him no, that I didn't need a servant and could handle my own luggage. But this was how Henry made money to care for his family and I was not going to let him be short changed. My friend was a good man and deserved to be treated better, but in this world of racial and social inequality there was only so much I could do for him. I'd offered him a job with my company's Vegas branch several times but he said that wouldn't be a fair way to get a job. He had his pride, but he wouldn't look down on presents for his children.

"They sure do," Henry replied wistfully. We entered the waiting first class elevator, Henry pushed the button, and the door shut. Once the door was shut he continued, "You have a visitor in your suite, Frank. He says you're expecting him."

"Yes," I grunted, "I hate to say it Henry, but this isn't a pleasure trip."

"I thought as much, you always wire ahead to let us know you're coming," Henry said sadly. "Is it bad?"

"I'm not sure Henry, but maybe if you have some sick days you should take them."

He nodded and said nothing. My friend was a soldier in Europe. He fought his way up the Italian Boot with General Clarke and never shirked his duty. Now he looked scared.

"I'll handle it Henry," I said reassuringly.

"If you need help, Frank, all you have to do is ask," he replied squaring his shoulders. "I might have more grey than black in my hair, but I can still sling a rifle and work the bolt."

I smiled sadly. Why were people always so ready to put themselves in danger for me?

Chapter Three

Now

In The Air

"Who's Vlad?" Susan asked stopping my story in mid-tale. It was something I loved and her teachers hated about her, she was never afraid to ask questions.

I had to fight back a grin at the look on her face when I told her.

"Dracula is real?" she asked in disbelief. "So you're THE Frankenstein, Zombies weren't invented by George Romero, and Count Dracula is real?!"

"He doesn't really like being called Dracula," I snickered. "He's always saying if he had a chance to meet Abraham Stoker he'd slap him upside the back of his head for making that his moniker."

"Fine, Vlad then," she said brushing my statement aside. "Frank what else is real?"

I took in a deep breath. "Werewolves, fairies, mythological gods and goddesses, monsters, demons, vampires, mummies, and just about any other nightmare creature you can think of."

She gawped at me open mouthed.

"They're not all bad," I continued. "Vlad is my friend and he's one of the good guys."

"He's killed so many people though," Susan said still in shock.

"When he was still human he was a leader at war against an unstoppable enemy," I said calmly. "That doesn't make the things he did right, but he thought he was saving his people. When he first changed, he couldn't always control his hunger. The stories of deaths from that time have multiplied exponentially over the centuries, but I know that he regrets what he did every single day."

"What about now?" Susan asked. She was as quick as always and her recovery from her initial shock was in full swing—I was filled with pride.

"There's a synthetic blood his company developed for medical use, he has employees who donate, and he has family he can feed from."

"Family?"

"He has a wife and three children," I answered. "His wife is a werewolf and their children are half and half."

"This is a lot to take in," Susan whispered burying her head into my chest. "Frank, who or what, is behind all this chaos?"

"That's a long story," I said guardedly. "I can tell you, but I'll need to stop the current one."

"No," she said, "wait until we're safe on the ground to tell me about it. Please finish the one about Vegas. Who was waiting for you when you got to your suite?"

I grinned at the memory. "I'm not easily surprised but when I opened the door..."

Chapter Four

December 1963

Sands High Roller Suite, Las Vegas

I opened the door and froze in shock. I'm not sure who I thought I'd find waiting for me, but the Chairman of the Board would not have been on my list in a thousand years.

"Get ya gear in here and shut the door, pally," the man said. His accent was pure East Coast Mid Atlantic. "And don't forget to tip Henry, he's a good man and has a family to think about."

Automatically I handed a grinning Henry four twenties.

"Remember what I said Mr. Castle, you need me and I'm there," Henry whispered before seeing himself out of the suite and closing the door.

"Sit down, pally, we have a lot to talk about," the

Chairman said indicating one of the oversized couches. "Drink?"

"Scotch, no ice," I said taking a seat and getting centered. "Fill the glass."

"Good man," he said approvingly. He handed me the drink and settled into his own seat.

"Mr. Sinatra-" I began but he cut me off.

"Call me Frank. Yeah, I know that's your name too but this is my town," he said with a grin before downing his drink. "That's smooth," he whistled. "You know the good stuff, pally."

"My father appreciated finer spirits," I said taking a slug of my own drink.

"Was he actually European royalty or was that just in the book?" the Chairman asked.

"How do you know who I am?" I asked guardedly.

"Vlad, told me," he said nodding. "When I contacted him and he told me he wasn't on the continent, he said he'd send you."

"Vlad has always talked too much," I muttered finishing my drink.

"Regardless," the Chairman continued dismissively, "we have a serious situation and we need help."

"Who are 'we', the Rat Pack?" I asked smiling.

"Hey, pally," Sinatra snapped, "we're not the Rat Pack, we're the Summit or the Clan, the Rat Pack are the other guys. "

"Alright," I said holding up a hand, "I meant no offense Frank. What are we dealing with?"

"Vampires," the man said. "A bunch of stinking vampires have the President of the United States in the desert."

"I watched the news before heading out from Chicago," I said confused. "President Johnson is in Europe."

"Not President Johnson," Sinatra said sadly. "President Kennedy. The goddamn blood suckers have Jack."

Nevada State Route 85

"President Kennedy died last month," I said. We were speeding in a cherry red Cadillac west of Vegas headed into the vast expanse of the dessert. "I watched it on TV, everyone did."

"Nah, that's just what those schmucks in DC want

everyone to think," the Chairman grumbled. "They want everyone to think that pasty Oswald killed him and they're hoping to use the whole thing to expand that mess in Southeast Asia."

"Okay, so what really happened?" I asked still trying to wrap my head around the idea that John Kennedy was still alive.

"They shot Jack," Sinatra said flatly, "that much is true. Four shooters and they still failed to kill him. Jack's a tough bastard."

"Alright, who shot him?"

"Have you heard of the DPA?" he asked. When he saw my blank expression he added, "Up until a few years ago they were Department 27."

"I know who they are," I growled.

"Well," he continued looking at me sideways, "then you know they're tricky bastards."

"They tried to kill President Kennedy?" I asked in disbelief. I wasn't a fan of the organization but I respected them, and this wasn't something I would have expected from them. It wasn't in their playbook at all.

"Oh God no, pally," Sinatra laughed. "Jack empowered them. He gave them the authority they'd been craving for a hundred years."

"Then who tried to kill him?" I asked now completely confused, it was a feeling I was not used to and I didn't enjoy it.

"The Order of the Black Light," the Chairman answered through clenched teeth. "This wasn't the first time they tried to whack Jack either."

"So they broke into the hospital and abducted him instead of just finishing him off?" I asked more confused than ever. I was starting to get mad at the lack of clear answers.

"Nah, pally, the Order took their shot and blew it, there was no way the Feds were gonna let them near Jack," Sinatra laughed.

"Then," I growled, "who kidnapped President Kennedy?"

"It was that son of a bitch, Humphrey Bogart!"

The Abandoned Barn

The Cadillac pulled into the open barn doors and the Chairman killed the engine.

"Um Frank," I said, "Humphrey Bogart died in 1957."

"Nah that was when he turned into a filthy blood sucker," he said throwing the door open and stepping out. "Old Bogey had the cancer and was willing to go to any length to stay alive. I'm not sure where he met the vamp that changed him, but it doesn't matter, in the end Bogey was dead and a monster now wears his skin. Since then he's been turning members of the Rat Pack into his own entourage through mind control and transformation."

"Dean, Sammy, and Peter are serving Bogart?" I asked finding the entire idea impossible. I'd hunted monsters with Dr. Watson and Sherlock Holmes under London, but this was hard for me to accept.

"No," Frank snapped, "I said the Rat Pack, the real Rat Pack—Errol Flynn, Nat King Cole, Mickey Rooney, Cesar Romero, Spencer Tracy, Cary Grant, and Rex Harrison."

"They're not all vampires," another voice said. "In fact I think Flynn and Cole are the only ones."

"But there are a lot of vampires under his control," a third voice added.

"But that's too many for just us to handle on our own. Which is why we asked Vlad for help, baby," the fourth and final voice finished.

Dean Martin, Peter Lawford, and Sammy Davis Jr. stood waiting for us at the entry to the barn.

Chapter Five

Now

In The Air

"Did that really happen?" Susan asked.

"Trust me, no one was more surprised than me," I said smiling at the memory of the four men readying themselves for battle. "But I swear, Susan, the Rat Pack was there waiting for me."

"I thought you said Mr. Sinatra said they weren't the Rat Pack?" she asked.

"Yeah," I laughed, "and he kept saying it until he died, but it doesn't change the reality that when people say the 'Rat Pack' that's who they think of."

"Frank, what's the Order of the..." she trailed off trying to remember the name I'd said.

"The Order of the Black Light," I said uncomfortably.

"Yeah, what's that? Are they like the Free Masons

or the Skull and Bones?"

"A little," I said heavily. "About the same as a camp fire is to a thermonuclear explosion."

Susan gulped.

Outside the snow and wind increased.

"The Order has been around a long time," I finally said. "There are tales tracing back to the halls of Atlantis and the plateau of Thule. As long as there has been a human race, there's been a version of the Order. They've been influencing events and manipulating the human race for a very long time."

"How do you know all of this?" Susan asked.

"I've spent most of my life researching and fighting them," I replied glumly. "They've hurt and killed a lot of people I love."

"Did they kill Alison?" she asked softly.

She knew about Alison, but she knew it hurt me to talk about her. I was never going to forget my wife and often talked of her freely, but I'd always been careful to speak of her in the proper time.

"Why was the Rat Pack so comfortable with the concept of vampires?" she asked changing the subject to something less painful.

"I asked and none of them would give me a

straight answer. In the seventies I got Sammy to tell me they had some kind of bad go in Mexico back in the fifties. Apparently that was how he lost his eye, but I never got details from any of them." I laughed remembering how drunk I'd had to get the man to say that much.

"So wait," she said backing the story up, "if this Order tried to have Kennedy assassinated then why didn't he just finish him off? And why did Bogart abduct him and keep him alive?"

"The Chairman never said Bogart wanted Kennedy dead," I said sadly. "I think in some weird and twisted way he thought he was helping him."

"So what did you do?" she asked snuggling back into me.

"I wasn't in charge," I chuckled. "The Chairman was running the show and I was content to just watch and wait."

Chapter Six

December 1963

West of Las Vegas

The Caddy came to a rumbling stop in front of the most dilapidated and ominous building I'd ever seen outside of Eastern Europe. The slanted three story brick and beam monstrosity reeked of evil.

"Yeah, this isn't the beginning of a horror movie," Dino said with a dark laugh before sliding out of the car. "When's old Boris Karloff, dressed up Frankenstein's monster, gonna come out and try to kill us?"

"Uh Dino," Sammy said joining jabbing him in the ribs. "Maybe you want to rethink that comparison baby."

"Sorry Frankie," Dean said looking at me and blushing. "I just meant it looks like something out of a

30's horror movie."

"Just don't let it happen again, Dino," I deadpanned.

All of the color washed out of his face, and the night went silent. The Chairman broke the tension with his raucous laughter. Sam and Peter both snapped their heads to look at Sinatra, but Dino never took his eyes off me and my unsmiling countenance.

"That's a good one, pally," the Chairman laughed. "Calm down and change ya panties Dino, Frankie's just razzing your berries."

I smiled and the tension broke.

The Rat Pack broke out into gales of laughter.

"That was a good one Frankie," Dino said punching me lightly in the arm. "It's not that easy to pull a fast one on me. You're alright buddy."

"Hey, baby," Sammy said still laughing, "you can hang with us any time. When we get back to the strip we're gonna make some memories."

"Yeah," Lawford whispered with the ghost of a smile, "but first we have to get my brother back."

"Quit being a wet rag—we'll get him, Peter," Dino said walking around to the back of the Caddy and popping the trunk. "First we have to suit up."

***

I have to admit I was impressed. They were a group of actors and entertainers, yet in that moment they looked like warriors. The men were already dressed in dark suits when we arrived from Sin City, now they'd added long leather coats, fedoras, and a ton of deadly weapons in all varieties. For a moment I was reminded of the cave in Tuscany, the last minutes before we cast the die and entered the darkness.

The night my life changed forever.

"We are chrome plated daddy-o," Dino whistled.

"They're up in that rats nest cruising for a bruisin'," Lawford said jacking a round into his shotgun. "We have some regulating to do."

"Remember," the Chairman said, "the vamps are fair game but the rest of those poor schmucks are being controlled. Shoot to wound, unless you have no other choice, capuche?"

There were nods and murmurs of agreement from the three men.

Then he turned to me. "Frankie, you're our ringer."

I crossed my arms over my chest and nodded.

"When we get in there big guy, your number one job is to find Jack," he continued checking the forty caliber colts strapped to his thighs. "We get Jack back at all costs."

"One way or another I'll find him," I replied.

"All right," the Chairman said addressing all of us. "We've all dealt with these blood suckers before and we know what they can do. It's gonna be hard, but ain't none of us a paper shaker!"

The three men cheered in agreement.

"Now let's get in there and rattle their cages and pound on some vamps."

Chapter Seven

Now

In The Air

"Did people really talk like that in real life?" Susan asked giggling. "I thought that was just in the movies and on the television."

"Do you really think your generation doesn't have a ton of weird slang?" I asked chuckling. "For that matter, when I was born children still learned Greek and Latin in school. Besides I'm editing out the worst of it as I tell it to you—if I recited it verbatim I'd have to stop and explain every other term to you."

She was laughing so hard now tears leaked from the corners of her eyes.

"I love you Frank," she said wiping her eyes.

"I love you, too," I said grinning. Despite all the chaos, death, and uncertainty I hadn't been this happy or content in a long time.

"Kiss me?" she said full of hope.

If I'd had thought about it I would have hesitated. Our age difference, our former relationship, and worry this would destroy our friendship, would have flooded my mind and killed the moment. If the moment had been killed I think things never would have progressed from the current level.

Thankfully I didn't think, I just lowered my head and kissed her.

Lips parted and soon the kiss grew more intense. She reached up and wrapped her arms around my neck pulling us even closer together. She was warm and filled with life, her touch made me feel young and new again. She made me feel alive.

"Is the door locked?" she asked breaking the kiss and breathing hard.

"Brenda," I said.

"Yes Frank?" the plane's computer responded.

"Secure cockpit," I answered with a grin.

Susan laughed and kissed me harder.

Clothes were shed without a second thought. Much like the plane, I was working on autopilot. I never stopped to consider any of it. I'd never allowed myself to imagine that she felt the same for me as I did for her, or that something like this could ever possibly happen. Now it was and nothing had ever felt this right.

I sat back in the pilot's chair and she approached me grinning wickedly. Long dark hair cascading over her shoulders as Susan straddled the same lap she'd been seeking the comfort of a bedtime story in only a moments earlier. She was light and agile, the touch of her flesh to mine sent electricity though my nerves.

"I've waited so long," she whispered leaning forward and kissing me on my cheek. "I have been in love with you for as long as I've known how to feel love."

I ran my hands down her bare back and was rewarded with a soft moan.

Her fingers traced one of the faded and ragged scars criss-crossing my body.

I went still with fear.

"Hey," she whispered, "I love you and want to know every inch of you so well I can recreate you in my mind. There is nothing for you to feel ashamed of or try to hide from me. I love you for you. For the man I know you are deep inside your large and caring heart, and for the selfless man I see when I look at you. I don't care if you have scars, we all have them, some of us just wear them on the outside."

I was shocked to feel hot tears building. It'd been a long time since I'd cried and not since Alison had I felt such unconditional acceptance and unconditional love.

Pressing her mouth to mine Susan reached between us and took me in her hand. I groaned into her open mouth and allowed her to assume all control of the moment. I wanted to be hers. I needed to belong to her.

"Oh God, yes," she moaned slipping me inside. "Oh, yes Frank."

We were no longer two separate beings—we were a single creature of passion and raw emotion. Time compressed into a moment and expanded into an eternity and it was perfect.

***

"Was it worth the wait?" I asked running my fingers through her damp hair.

We were curled up in the pilot's chair, wrapped in a blanket from the cockpit supply closet, enjoying the afterglow of our coupling. I knew we'd soon have to return to facing the dark reality we're currently living in, but for the moment she was my entire universe.

"I would have waited forever," she murmured. "I'm sleepy for real now, Frank."

"Do you want me to finish the story?" I asked.

Susan nodded.

Chapter Eight

December 1963

The Vampire House

The front door was old and dry rotted from so many years in the desert. My booted foot slamming into it caused the door to be ripped from the frame. The splintered wooden panels flew apart and disappeared into the darkness of the interior.

"Where are they Frank?" Dino asked the Chairman shining a flashlight into the building.

"Maybe they don't know we're here, baby," Sammy answered sweeping his Tommy Gun back and forth before crossing the threshold in front of me.

"They know we're here," I said following him in. "They knew before the Caddy stopped in front of this death trap," I said.

"Of course we did!" a familiar voice said from the top of the houses central grand staircase.

Four flashlights turned toward the source of the words.

My preternatural vision allowed me to see the room like it was mid day and lit up for Sunday lunch. On the second floor landing Humphrey Bogart, Errol Flynn, and Nat King Cole stood looking at us.

"Hand over my brother and we can all walk away from this still thinking," Peter said aiming the barrel of his shotgun at the trio.

"I don't think so," Bogey replied. "Hey Frank where's Joey Bishop? I figured he was permanently glued to your ass."

"Joey's watching the store, pally," the Chairman replied drawing one of his pistols. "Where's the rest of your crew? I was under the impression the rest of your Pack was gonna be here, I was looking forward to pounding on some of those mooks."

"We sent then back to town," Errol laughed. "Like we need them getting in the way while we handle five normal's armed with pop guns and crosses."

"Yeah," Nat agreed, "the only question is how this is gonna go down."

"What do you mean?" the Chairman asked. "The way this goes down is you either give us Jack or we take him from you."

The three vampires laughed.

The laughter might have been real and my new friends may have believed it, but I was observing the situation. Things didn't look, smell, or feel right. The house smelled of death, not the normal death associated with vampires but like recent death, human death. The three of them looked disheveled, it was almost an unnatural law that vampire tended to be impeccable in their grooming unless they'd gone crazy and these three didn't look crazy.

"No Frank", Bogey continued not paying me any attention. "The only choices are do we come down there, tear you apart and feast on you, or do you join us and be turned."

The men around me tensed for battle as their answer.

"When did they come?" I asked.

All heads, both human and vampire, turned toward me.

"When did the Order figure out you secreted President Kennedy away from the hospital in Dallas?" I pressed on. "Did they kill your friends or were you able to get them out of here before you slaughtered the Order's agents?"

Nat and Errol gawped, but Bogey laughed sadly. "We got the rest of the Rat Pack out before those thugs showed up. I don't know what they thought they were going to be dealing with but they weren't expecting three of us."

"Give us the President," I said.

"I don't know who you are big guy, but if these punks wanted to scare us they would've sent in Dracula," Bogey laughed.

"They called him," I said with a laugh, "and he sent me!"

I've said before, and I will probably say it a hundred more times before I'm finished telling my story, but I move very fast. Vlad moves faster than me, but he is one of the oldest of his kind. These were very young vampires, practically children, and they were not faster.

"Get him!" Bogey screamed.

He was the most dangerous, that was obvious with every movement, so he was my target. I didn't even question whether my friends would do their part and wasn't surprised when the gunfire began. My fist impacted with Bogey's chest and knocked him into the landing's back wall.

"What are you?" the vampire snarled in shock.

"I am creature even more fantastical than you, Bogey," I said grinning. It'd been a while since I could unload my full power without fear of bystander casualties.

Below me the battle raged four on two. The conversation amongst my friends was background noise, but as with all things I heard it all.

"Get him Frank!" Dino yelled unloading with his shotgun.

The weapons were loaded with combination silver and wood rounds, which meant any hit with them were going to be hurting a lot.

"I see him, Dino," the Chairman replied. "Get your ass over here Flynn so I can plug it!" the demand was punctuated by his dual wielded forty-fives roaring to life.

Sammy's Chicago Piano filled the dilapidated house with the roar of manmade thunder. It was followed closely by the screams of a vampire, I assumed it was Nat, punctured by dozens of rounds designed to hurt his kind.

"Where's my brother?!" Lawford yelled adding his own thunder to the cacophony below.

"Get the stakes, ya mugs!" the Chairman

ordered.

I smiled. My new friends could handle it.

"Where's the President?" I demanded advancing on Bogey.

Bogart sniffed and looked at me. "What are you? You smell wrong."

I punched and the vampire dodged resulting in my fist being lodged in the lathe and plaster wall. Grunting I wrenched it free and turned just in time for Humphrey Bogart to punch my square in the face. It hurt and I knew that despite the minimal surface blood in my skin there'd be a bruise.

"You are wrong," he said landing another one on my chest. The little bastard was fast and he threw a decent punch, I thought as I stumbled back into the wall.

He threw a third punch and I caught it with my left hand in mid air.

"Look who's talking," I said swinging my right arm and catching him in the side of his head. Vampires are not invulnerable, they simply heal so fast they might as well be. But a vampire this young couldn't heal faster than I could attack.

Below the sounds of battle were reaching a

crescendo.

Fists and feet flew as I backed Bogey into the corner by hitting and kicking as fast as I could. The vampire attempted to break the engagement a hundred times but it soon became apparent that other than his vampire powers, he had no real fighting skills. I allowed the red rage of battle to descend and lost myself in the assault. Not since Tuscany had I allowed myself to lose myself in my inner monster.

"Frankie!" the Chairman said from behind me. "Frankie, we've won you can stop."

I whipped around and found myself looking at the Rat Pack. The four men were arrayed on the top step watching me. They were covered in gore and dirt but they were all alive. My eyes took in the sight of the two vampires staked at the bottom of the stairs and urged my rage to seep away.

"You okay, baby?" Sammy asked, the smoking barrel of his Tommy Gun aimed at Bogey. "We handled the light work," he added with a dark laugh.

I nodded backing away from the smashed and rapidly healing body of Humphrey Bogart. I always felt sick after a fight and that day was no exception.

"Good work, Frankie," the Chairman said, "but we need this bum talking so he can tell us where Jack is."

That was when Bogey started laughing through a mouth full of blood and broken teeth.

Chapter Nine

Now

In The Air

Susan slept soundly despite the heavy snow. I moved her to the copilot seat and wrapped her in the blanket. Instead of slackening, the storm was getting worse and as a result the strain on the engines was worse than I'd anticipated when we left the burning ruins of Ann Arbor. I needed to find a place to rest them before crossing Lake Superior.

"Is there anyone out there?" I asked quietly after keying the mic on my radio. I'd been broadcasting on all the aviation frequencies since finishing my tale and other than a few isolated broadcasters besieged by the dead, I'd raised no one.

"Damn," I muttered setting the mic back in its cradle.

I eyed the dangerously high reactor temperature

gauge and shuddered internally. I looked at the digital map on the console and sighed in resignation. There was one option I could try but it'd been a long time since I'd dealt with them.

"Nikola and Albert trusted them," I muttered reaching for the mic and hesitating. "But Gammell thought they were not to be trusted. Of course the old duffer saw conspiracies everywhere."

Brenda shuddered and I picked the mic back up. Switching to the special frequency I spoke, "This Franklin Castle to Institute Air Traffic Control, please respond." I unkeyed and waited. I didn't have to wait long.

"Mr. Castle this is Institute Air Traffic Control," a tight female voice answered. "Professor Davis never returned."

"Are we really doing this?" I asked. "The world is ending and you're still doing codes and counter codes. I think the Order has made its damn move, the time for secrecy is over."

"Professor Davis never returned," the woman countered icily.

"The cables broke and the portal closed," I sighed in irritated resignation giving my counter response.

"Good enough? I have a plane full of refugees and a reactor being pushed to its limits. I need a safe place to set down and rest the engines, are you secure?"

"Yes, Mr. Castle we are currently secure," the woman continued not sounding nearly as tense, but not exactly welcoming exactly. "I am lighting up the secondary runway, I will only be keeping it illuminated until you touch down. I have no desire to attract trouble to us, we've had more than enough already."

"Is Director Pemberton on the campus?" I asked adjusting Brenda to switch into VTOL mode.

The woman made a choked sound before answering. When she did she sounded decidedly less aggressive. "No, Director Pemberton was in Arkham when this all started, we've had no contact with him."

Damn, I thought. I'd been hoping Harold Pemberton would be able to help me get things organized. If he'd been in Arkham when the dead rose I prayed he died quickly. "I'll need to speak to whoever's in charge when I land, I have information they're gonna need if Miskatonic has been knocked out of the game."

"What game?" she asked resigned. "We just had our collective asses kicked."

"No," I replied brining Brenda into a hover over the runway and beginning my decent. "We lost the first battle but this war is just getting started."

On the Ground

"What is this place Frank?" Susan asked.

The rest of the passengers were remaining on Brenda until I decided if the situation was safe. Andy was less than happy about it, but when I asked him to watch Brenda's thermostat for me, he was pleased to have an important job. The snow was three feet high expect for a few walkways and the short secondary runway. I began to answer Susan but someone beat me to it. It was a man's voice I hadn't heard in over fifty years.

"Welcome the Marquette Institute of Thaumaturlogical Research," he said.

We both turned to see who was speaking. Susan was rendered silent by shock, me by irritation. This was a complication I didn't need.

"We just call it The Institute," John Fitzgerald Kennedy said in his educated Bostonian accent. Smiling at me and exposing his tiny fangs he added, "How have you been Frank?"

"All thing considered Jack, I'm alright," I responded guardedly. "What are you doing out here?"

"You told Tamara you needed to talk to the person in charge, well here I am."

About The Author

Josh is a native of the Metro Detroit region of Michigan and currently calls Dayton, Ohio home. He cut his writing teeth in the role-playing game (RPG) industry, working for companies such as Palladium Books and Third Eye Games. Josh married his wife Karen in 1996. They have six children and two grandchildren. Josh writes in a variety of genres, but the majority of his books are in the realms of science fiction and horror.

www.ingramcontent.com/pod-product-compliance
Lightning Source LLC
LaVergne TN
LVHW031345150826
845673LV00009B/2874